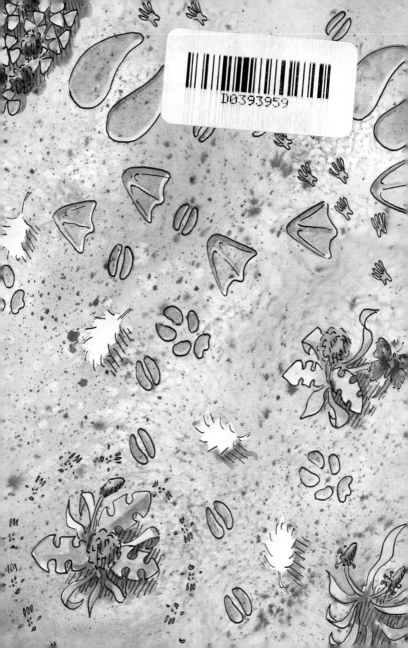

*This book is for my dad, Roland Smith,
who told us all about Bella and Gertie.*

A catalogue record for this book is available from the British Library

Published by Ladybird Books Ltd
A subsidiary of the Penguin Group
A Pearson Company
First published by Ladybird Books Ltd MCMXCVI   This edition MCMXCVII

LADYBIRD and the device of a Ladybird are trademarks of
Ladybird Books Ltd Loughborough Leicestershire UK

Text © Geraldine Taylor MCMXCVI
Illustrations © Ladybird Books Ltd MCMXCVI

The author/artist have asserted their moral rights

BELLA & GERTIE

by Geraldine Taylor
illustrated by Guy Parker Rees

Ladybird

The whole farmyard was in uproar. The geese were hissing, the ducks' feathers were standing on end and the donkey had 'hee-hawed' so many times he was hoarse!

Something dreadful had happened during the night. The hen house was empty and every single hen had vanished without a trace.

All the animals were calling for Bella and Gertie, the world-famous private detectives, to find the culprit and solve the mystery.

"We'll go to the scene of the crime and look for clues," said Bella. "But we'll have to make sure that nobody sees us."

"I'll put on my dark glasses," said Gertie. "Then no one can see me."

"And I'll wear my detective hat," said Bella. "And no one will be able to see me either."

"I've found a clue," said Gertie. "Someone has opened the hen house door. We must find out who did it."

"I'll ask the questions," said Bella, "and you listen to the answers, Gertie."

"*I* didn't open the door," said the horse.

"*I* didn't open the door," said the bull.

"*We* didn't open the door," said the sheep.

"And it certainly wasn't *me*," said Foxy. "I've hurt my paw – I can't go round opening doors. Look how Mrs Foxy's bandaged me up!"

"These muddy footprints are a clue," said Bella. "We'll have to ask you all to show us your feet."

"They're not *my* footprints," said the rabbit.

"They're not *my* footprints," said the horse.

"They're not *our* footprints," said the geese.

"Well, they certainly aren't *my* footprints," said Foxy. "Look, I have to wear my black boots. Mrs Foxy gets cross if I come indoors with muddy paws."

"Did any of you hear strange noises in the middle of the night?" asked Bella.

"We did!" cried the sheep. "We heard a horrible howl and we almost jumped out of our wool!"

"That's a clue!" said Gertie.
"We must find out who howls in the middle of the night."

"*I* can't howl," said the goat.

"*I* can't howl," said the turkey.

"*I* can't howl," said the donkey.

"And *I* certainly can't howl," croaked Foxy. "I've got a dreadful sore throat. Mrs Foxy makes me wear this scarf to keep it warm."

Bella and Gertie examined the ground with their magnifying glasses. Suddenly, Gertie cried, "I've found a trail!"

Sure enough, there was a trail of feathers leading from the hen house through the gate and into the field.

"Follow those feathers!" cried Bella.

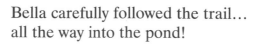

Bella carefully followed the trail... all the way into the pond!

"Someone is trying to make us look ridiculous," said Bella. "Well, it won't work. We're world-famous private detectives. We'll set a trap."

That evening, the farmyard was in uproar again because there was a notice on the hen house door. It said:

THEEVES
KEEP
OUT
6 NEU HENZ
IN HEER

"How could the farmer get new hens when we don't know what's happened to the old ones?" cried the donkey.

"Why can't Bella and Gertie solve the mystery and get our friends back?" hissed the geese.

But Bella and Gertie said nothing.

That night, the cow detectives kept watch at either end of the hen house…

Suddenly, in the moonlight, a shadow crept up to the hen house and carefully lifted the latch. Gertie slammed the door shut and cried. "I've trapped the criminal – it's a shadow! I've never trusted shadows!"

But Bella peeped through the hole in the hen house roof and cried…

"It's FOXY! It's FOXY pretending to be a shadow. It's Foxy without his boots, and without his scarf and HE'S GOT A GREAT BIG SACK."

"There aren't any new hens, Foxy!" said Gertie. "We've caught you in our trap! What do you say about that?"

"You've got nasty, suspicious minds," said Foxy, sulkily. "I've brought a sackful of *presents* for the new hens. Let me out, I'm going home to Mrs Foxy. *She* knows what a kind, generous fox I am…"

"You aren't going anywhere until you tell us where you've hidden the hens," said Bella. "If you DON'T tell us, we'll go and get the farmer and you know what *he'll* do."

Foxy snarled, "They're in the old barn. I was keeping them for my birthday – a hen for every year of my age. Mrs Foxy was going to make such a wonderful stew."

And with that he jumped out of the hen house and ran home, giving the loudest, foxiest howl that anyone had ever heard.

The animals cheered when Bella and Gertie brought the hens home.
They all agreed how lucky they were that the most famous private detectives in the world lived in a cow shed on their farm.

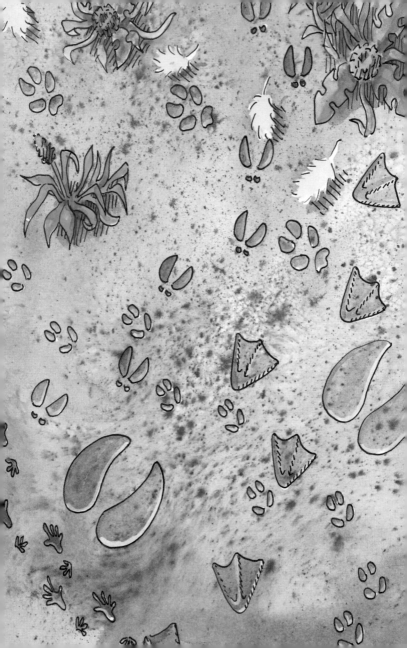